Humphrey's

Bedtime

To Georgia Lottie
Love Mum x

PUFFIN BOOKS

Published by the Penguin Group
Penguin Books Ltd, 27 Wrights Lane, London W8 5TZ, England
Penguin Putnam Inc., 375 Hudson Street, New York, New York 10014, USA
Penguin Books Australia Ltd, Ringwood, Victoria, Australia
Penguin Books Canada Ltd, 10 Alcorn Avenue, Toronto, Ontario, Canada M4V 3B2
Penguin Books India (P) Ltd, 11 Community Centre, Panchsheel Park, New Delhi — 110 017, India
Penguin Books (NZ) Ltd, Cnr Rosedale and Airborne Roads, Albany, Auckland, New Zealand
Penguin Books (South Africa) (Pty) Ltd, 5 Watkins Street, Denver Ext 4, Johannesburg 2094, South Africa

Penguin Books Ltd, Registered Offices: Harmondsworth, Middlesex, England

On the World Wide Web at: www.penguin.com

First published by Viking 2000
Published in Puffin Books 2001
1 3 5 7 9 10 8 6 4 2

Copyright © Sally Hunter, 2000
All rights reserved

The moral right of the author/illustrator has been asserted

Printed at Oriental Press, Dubai, U.A.E.

British Library Cataloguing in Publication Data
A CIP catalogue record for this book is available from the British Library

ISBN 0—140—56784—4

To find out more about Humphrey's world, visit the web site at:
www.humphreys-corner.com

Humphrey's

Bedtime

Sally Hunter

PUFFIN BOOKS

It was Baby's bedtime...
He had to go to bed first
because he was the smallest.

"Night, night."

"I am allowed to stay
up very…very late,"
said Lottie.

"That's because I am The Biggest…"

"...and that's what happens
when you are The Biggest."

"Bathtime," called Mummy.

Humphrey made big bubble mountains...

...and magic potions.

He had a lovely time.

But... when it was Lottie's
turn for her bath, she said...
"I don't have time for a bath.
My babies are soooo dirty.
They need a good wash."

And...

"I don't go to bed yet.
I am a BIG GIRL."

"Nearly done, Bear."

"Jim-jams on."

"Supper time ..." called Mummy.

Humphrey had hot milk
and buttery toast.

He felt warm and cosy in his tummy.

Mop liked his too.

But Lottie didn't want her supper.
She said...
"I don't have time for supper.
My babies keep complaining
they are hungry."

And...

"I don't go to bed yet...
I am a BIG GIRL."

"Eat it all up and you will grow
big and strong."

"neigh...neigghh...up the wooden hill."

"Story time," said Mummy.

It was Humphrey's favourite book.
He liked the pictures and the
magic fairies.

"Once upon a time,
there lived a little
pixie at the
bottom of the
garden..."

Humphrey was all snuggly...

...and sleepy.

But Lottie didn't want her story.
She said...
"My babies are only little,
they are very tired.
I must tuck them up in bed."

And...

"I don't go to bed yet.
I am a BIG GIRL."

But Lottie was having problems
with her babies.

Lulu was being silly…

...Trevor wouldn't wear his
pyjamas properly...

Barry wouldn't lie down...

and Bear had got lost.

Lottie felt all hot...

...and CROSS!

"What's all this...?" said Daddy.

"Come on, my Funny Little Girl."

"Off we go ..."

"...to..."

"...bed."